I0766462

Framing the Warrior: Bruce Lee's Golden Harvest Photo Session

FOREWORD

THE WARRIOR WITHIN

THE "WARRIOR" PHOTO SHOOT HAS LONG BEEN AMONG MY VERY FAVOURITE IMAGES OF BRUCE LEE. OVER THE YEARS, I HAVE COLLECTED MANY OF THESE PORTRAITS, ALWAYS STRUCK BY THEIR POWER AND MYSTERY. THE EXACT NUMBER OF PHOTOGRAPHS TAKEN THAT DAY IS NOT CERTAIN, BUT WITHIN THESE PAGES, YOU WILL FIND WHAT I BELIEVE TO BE A LARGE MAJORITY OF THE SESSION CARRIED OUT AT THE GOLDEN HARVEST STUDIO IN HONG KONG.

THE MATERIAL SURVIVES LARGELY IN THE FORM OF CONTACT SHEETS — STRIPS OF FILM THAT CAPTURE SEQUENCES OF SHOTS TAKEN IN QUICK SUCCESSION. SOME FRAMES SHOW BRUCE FROZEN IN NEARLY IDENTICAL POSES, WITH ONLY THE SMALLEST SHIFT IN EXPRESSION OR MOVEMENT BETWEEN THEM. SOME SHOTS ARE MISSING ENTIRELY, SUGGESTING THAT PERHAPS THERE MAY BE SEVERAL MORE CONTACT SHEETS. EVEN IN THE SHEETS, SOME WERE CUT AWAY FROM THE ORIGINAL ROLL. WHAT REMAINS, HOWEVER, ALLOWS US TO TRACE A VISUAL TIMELINE OF THAT DAY, AND TO COMPARE IT WITH THE IMAGES MANY FANS AND COLLECTORS HAVE GATHERED FOR THEIR OWN ARCHIVES.

I HAVE ALSO INCLUDED A SMALL SELECTION OF PHOTOGRAPHS FROM THE SEPARATE SHAW BROTHERS SESSION THAT I HAVE COLLECTED, BUT THE HEART OF THIS BOOK LIES IN GOLDEN HARVEST'S "WARRIOR" PORTRAITS. IMPORTANTLY, NO AI MANIPULATION OR DIGITAL ALTERATION HAS BEEN APPLIED HERE. THE PHOTOGRAPHS ARE PRESENTED IN THEIR RAW, UNTAMPERED FORM, JUST AS THEY WERE ORIGINALLY SHOT. TO MY KNOWLEDGE, THIS IS THE FIRST TIME THEY HAVE BEEN ASSEMBLED IN A SINGLE VOLUME, PROVIDING A RECORD OF THE SESSION THAT TOOK PLACE THAT DAY.

THE CLEAREST OFFICIAL DOCUMENTATION OF THESE PORTRAITS COMES FROM GOLDEN HARVEST'S OWN POSTHUMOUS TRIBUTE, BRUCE LEE: THE MAN AND THE LEGEND (1973). RELEASED SHORTLY AFTER BRUCE'S UNTIMELY DEATH, THE DOCUMENTARY INCORPORATED FRAGMENTS OF THE STUDIO SHOOT, REVEALING HIM IN UNFAMILIAR GUISES: A BLIND JAPANESE SWORDSMAN, A STOIC WARRIOR ARMED WITH TRADITIONAL WEAPONS, AND MYTHIC MARTIAL FIGURES THAT SEEMED TO BELONG TO FILMS NEVER MADE. FOR MANY AUDIENCES, THIS WAS THE FIRST PROOF THAT LEE HAD POSED FOR SUCH EXTRAORDINARY STILLS.

Framing the Warrior: Bruce Lee's Golden Harvest Photo Session

In the decades that followed, the photographs circulated widely among collectors and enthusiasts, often under evocative titles such as Dragon of Jade or The Blind Swordsman. These names added an air of mystery but were never tied to any verified screenplay or film in development. Instead, they became part of the mythology surrounding Bruce Lee, a mythology deepened by his sudden passing in 1973. Every stray image became a tantalizing "what if," a glimpse of a project cut short or a character never realized.

More recently, official archival releases — such as Arrow Video's Bruce Lee at Golden Harvest box set — have returned these portraits to public view in restored quality, affirming their place in the studio's history. Yet it is only now, through the effort of gathering these raw images in one place, that we can truly appreciate the scope of the session.

The Golden Harvest portraits are more than curiosities. They reveal Bruce Lee's restless imagination, his ability to embody not just the martial artist we know from his films, but also a broader range of archetypes — timeless warriors who transcend genre and culture. They also reflect the studio's promotional strategies and the way star images were crafted in Hong Kong's cinema industry of the early 1970s.

Ultimately, these photographs stand as both historical record and artistic experiment. They are a window into Bruce's creative process and into the studio system that sought to capture and preserve his image. Seen together, they remind us of Lee's unique gift: whether on film or in still photography, he could project myth, intensity, and charisma in a single frame.

It is with great pride that I present these images in The Warrior Within. May they offer both fans and scholars alike a deeper appreciation of Bruce Lee, not only as a film star, but as an artist continually exploring new identities — even in the still silence of a studio portrait.

— Ricky

THE WARRIOR WITHIN

IN THE EARLY 1970S, AS BRUCE LEE WAS SHAPING THE FILMS THAT WOULD DEFINE HIS LEGACY, GOLDEN HARVEST ARRANGED A STUDIO PHOTO SESSION UNLIKE ANY OTHER. IT WAS HERE, IN HONG KONG, THAT LEE STEPPED BEFORE THE CAMERA NOT IN HIS FAMILIAR SCREEN ROLES BUT IN AN ARRAY OF STRIKING COSTUMES AND WITH CAREFULLY CHOSEN PROPS: A BLIND JAPANESE SWORDSMAN, A STOIC WARRIOR POISED WITH TRADITIONAL WEAPONS, AND OTHER ARCHETYPAL GUISES THAT HINTED AT STORIES NEVER BROUGHT TO THE SCREEN.

FOR DECADES, FANS AND COLLECTORS HAVE DEBATED THE MEANING OF THESE IMAGES. WERE THEY PROMOTIONAL STILLS FOR A SECRET PROJECT? A TEASER FOR A NEW MARTIAL-ARTS EPIC THAT NEVER MATERIALIZED? OR SIMPLY A CREATIVE PHOTO SESSION DESIGNED TO EXPLORE LEE'S RANGE OF PERSONAS AND TO FEED GOLDEN HARVEST'S PROMOTIONAL MACHINE? THE TRUTH APPEARS TO SIT SOMEWHERE IN BETWEEN.

WHAT CAN BE ESTABLISHED IS THAT THESE PORTRAITS WERE PART OF A GOLDEN HARVEST STUDIO SHOOT, MOST LIKELY ORGANIZED AROUND 1973. THE SESSION PRODUCED COSTUME AND PROP TEST PHOTOGRAPHS—STUDIO PORTRAITS RATHER THAN PRODUCTION STILLS—CAPTURING BRUCE AT A MOMENT OF EXPERIMENTATION. GOLDEN HARVEST WAS INVESTING HEAVILY IN HIS STAR POWER, AND LEE HIMSELF WAS THINKING FAR BEYOND A SINGLE FILM. THE STILLS PROVIDED A WAY TO IMAGINE NEW CHARACTERS, TO EXPLORE MARTIAL ARCHETYPES, AND TO TEST HOW AUDIENCES MIGHT RESPOND TO BRUCE EMBODYING DIFFERENT TRADITIONS OF THE WARRIOR.

THE WARRIOR WITHIN

SOME OF THE IMAGES RESURFACED SOON AFTER IN GOLDEN HARVEST'S DOCUMENTARY BRUCE LEE: THE MAN AND THE LEGEND (1973). LATER THEY APPEARED IN PROMOTIONAL COLLECTIONS AND, IN MODERN TIMES, IN ARCHIVAL BOX SETS SUCH AS BRUCE LEE AT GOLDEN HARVEST. COLLECTORS HAVE OFTEN ATTACHED NAMES SUCH AS "THE DRAGON OF JADE" OR "BLIND SWORDSMAN" TO THE SESSION, BUT NO VERIFIABLE PRODUCTION RECORD CONFIRMS THOSE TITLES. INSTEAD, IT SEEMS LIKELY THE SESSION WAS CONCEIVED AS A MIXTURE OF STUDIO PUBLICITY AND CREATIVE EXPLORATION, LEAVING US WITH PORTRAITS THAT FEEL LIKE FRAGMENTS OF UNMADE FILMS.

TODAY, THESE PHOTOGRAPHS HOLD A UNIQUE PLACE IN BRUCE LEE'S VISUAL LEGACY. THEY ARE NEITHER CASUAL SNAPSHOTS NOR FAMILIAR FILM STILLS, BUT CAREFULLY STAGED STUDIO IMAGES THAT REVEAL BRUCE'S WILLINGNESS TO SLIP INTO DIFFERENT IDENTITIES. THEY ALSO UNDERLINE THE COLLABORATIVE POWER OF GOLDEN HARVEST AT THE HEIGHT OF LEE'S FAME: A STUDIO EAGER TO PRESENT THEIR STAR NOT JUST AS AN ACTOR IN A ROLE, BUT AS A TIMELESS WARRIOR WHOSE APPEAL TRANSCENDED GENRE AND TRADITION.

FOR THE HISTORIAN AND THE FAN ALIKE, THE GOLDEN HARVEST PHOTO SESSION IS A REMINDER OF BRUCE LEE'S RESTLESS IMAGINATION. EVEN WHEN NO CAMERA WAS ROLLING ON A SET, HE APPROACHED THE LENS WITH INTENSITY, EMBODYING CHARACTERS THAT HINTED AT WORLDS BEYOND THE FILMS WE KNOW. THESE PORTRAITS ARE THEREFORE NOT JUST PROMOTIONAL CURIOSITIES—THEY ARE WINDOWS INTO LEE'S CREATIVE PROCESS, AND INTO THE STUDIO SYSTEM THAT SOUGHT TO HARNESS AND PRESERVE HIS LEGEND.

THE WARRIOR WITHIN
INTERPRETING THE IMAGES

To dismiss the Golden Harvest session as "just a photo shoot" is to underestimate its significance. These images reveal several important aspects of Bruce Lee's creative life:

Lee as Myth-Maker: Even when not acting in a film, Lee approached the camera with intensity, embodying personas that transcended specific narratives. He understood the power of the still image to construct myth.

The Studio System at Work: Golden Harvest used portrait sessions as tools of experimentation and marketing. They illustrate the ways in which Hong Kong studios managed star images not only through films but also through photography.

Cultural Crossroads: By depicting Lee as both Chinese warrior and Japanese swordsman, the portraits symbolized a pan-Asian martial identity. They reflected the regional exchange of cultural forms at a time when Hong Kong cinema was gaining global reach.

THE SESSION: BETWEEN PUBLICITY AND EXPERIMENT

Promotional Material: The stills could serve as generic promotional images, adaptable to international magazines, lobby displays, or future advertising campaigns.

Conceptual Experimentation: They offered a way to explore Bruce's potential in roles outside his established "avenger" persona — perhaps even to test the viability of a film in the swordplay or samurai subgenre.

Star Image Management: By placing Lee in archetypal guises, the studio reinforced his versatility and mythic qualities, emphasizing that he could embody not just a kung fu fighter, but a universal warrior figure.

CONTACT SHEET 1:
32 PHOTOGRAPHS

1528
26A
27

KODAK TRI X PAN FILM
1529
1530
1533
1537
1538
1542
1543
1547
→26A
→30A
→31A
→35A
FILM
→3
→3A
→7
8
→8A
12

1539
KODAK SAFET
29A
30
1532
30 A
1533
31A
32
3
8A
9
9A
10
10A
11
11A
12
12

1528
1529
KODAK TRI X PAN FILM
1530
1531
KODAK SAFETY FILM
1532
→29A
→30
KODAK SAFETY FILM
1536
1538
→34A
→35
→30A
→3
1537
→35A

KODAK TRI X
1548
12A →33
35A
TRI 9X PAN
LM
1542
KODAK SAFETY FILM
7A
11A
11
1548
KODAK
8
12A
10A
13
1559
10
13A
15
15A
17A
13
KODAK TRI X PAN
KODAK SAFETY FILM
1553
1554

CONTACT SHEET 2: 35 PHOTOGRAPHS

KODAK SAFETY FILM
8A
8
7A
7
6A
6

头条 @力道塾

CONTACT SHEET 3:
32 PHOTOGRAPHS

KODAK TRI X PAN
1529
27A
28
1528
26A
27

27A
28
KODAK TRI X PAN FILM
1534
32A
33
KODAK TRI X PAN FILM
28A
29
1535
33A
FILM
1533
31A
32

KODAK TRI-X PAN FILM
KODAK SAFETY FILM
KODAK TRI-X PAN FILM
1538
1539
1540
KODAK TRI-X PAN
1548
1553

1528
1529
1530
1531
1532
1543
KODA
8
8A
1548
1549
1550
1551
1552

1545
SAFETY FILM
546
3
11A
7A
9A
11
KODAK TRI X PAN FILM
1548
1549
KODAK TRI X PAN FILM
544
8
9A
11A
12
12A
1551
1552

28A
29
29A
30
KODAK SAFETY FILM
1535
1536
1547
1548
8
8A
9
9
KODAK TRI X PAN FILM
1548
1549
12
12A

KODAK SAFETY FILM
26A 27 28A 29 29A 30 30A
1533 1535 1536 1537
14A
1550
KODAK
3
154
1549
8 8A 9 9A
KODAK TRI X PAN FILM
1548 1549
15 15A

11
11A
12
12A
SAFETY FILM
1551
1552
26A
153
31A
153
3
3A
KODAK
1543
7A
154
7
7A
8
8A
KODAK TRI X
1548
12
12A
1552

13
13A
KODAK TRI X PAN FI
1553
18
18A
14
14A
1554
19
19A
20A
20

1557
22
22A
KODAK TRI-X PAN FILM
1558
23
23A
1559
24A
24

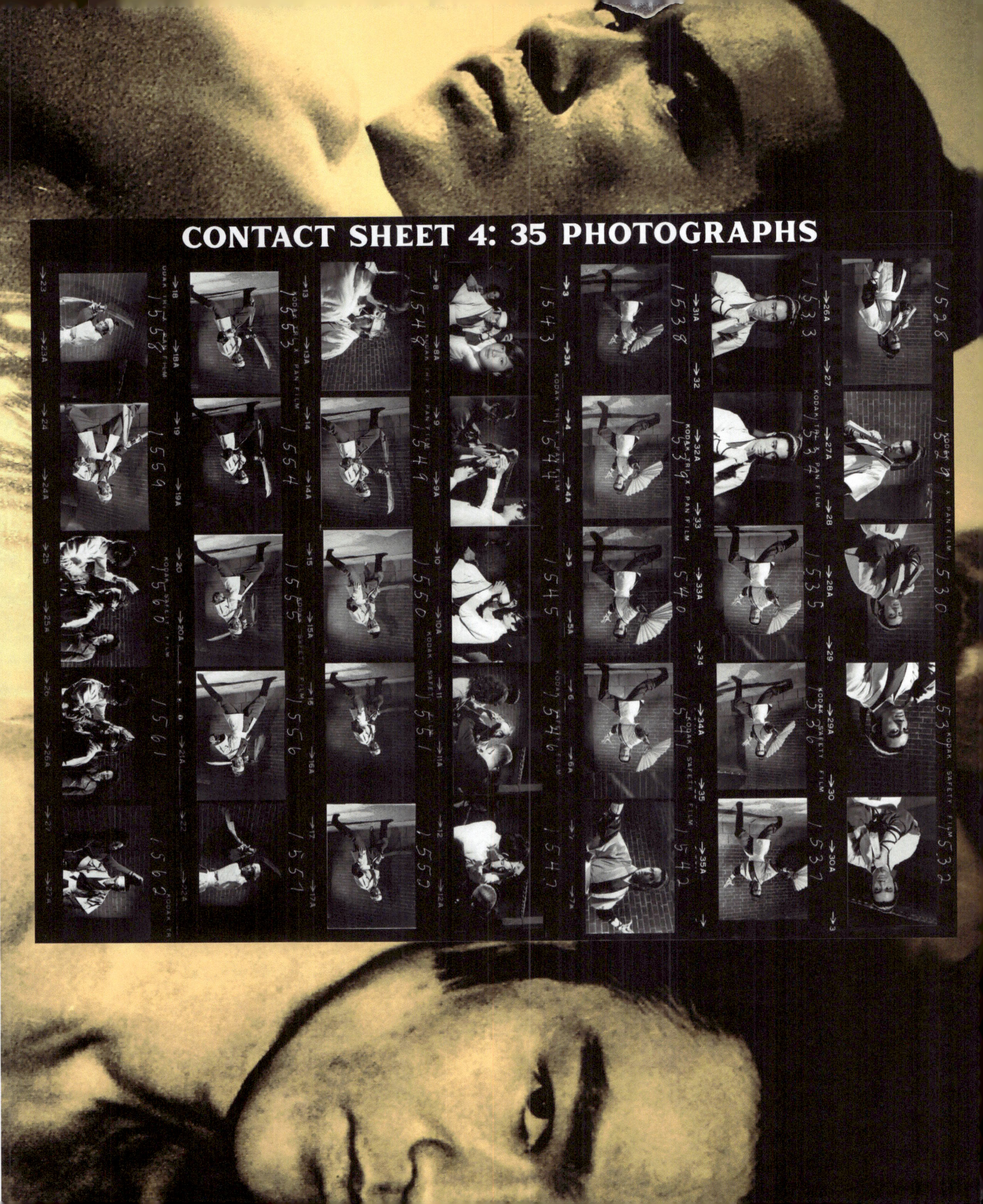
CONTACT SHEET 4: 35 PHOTOGRAPHS

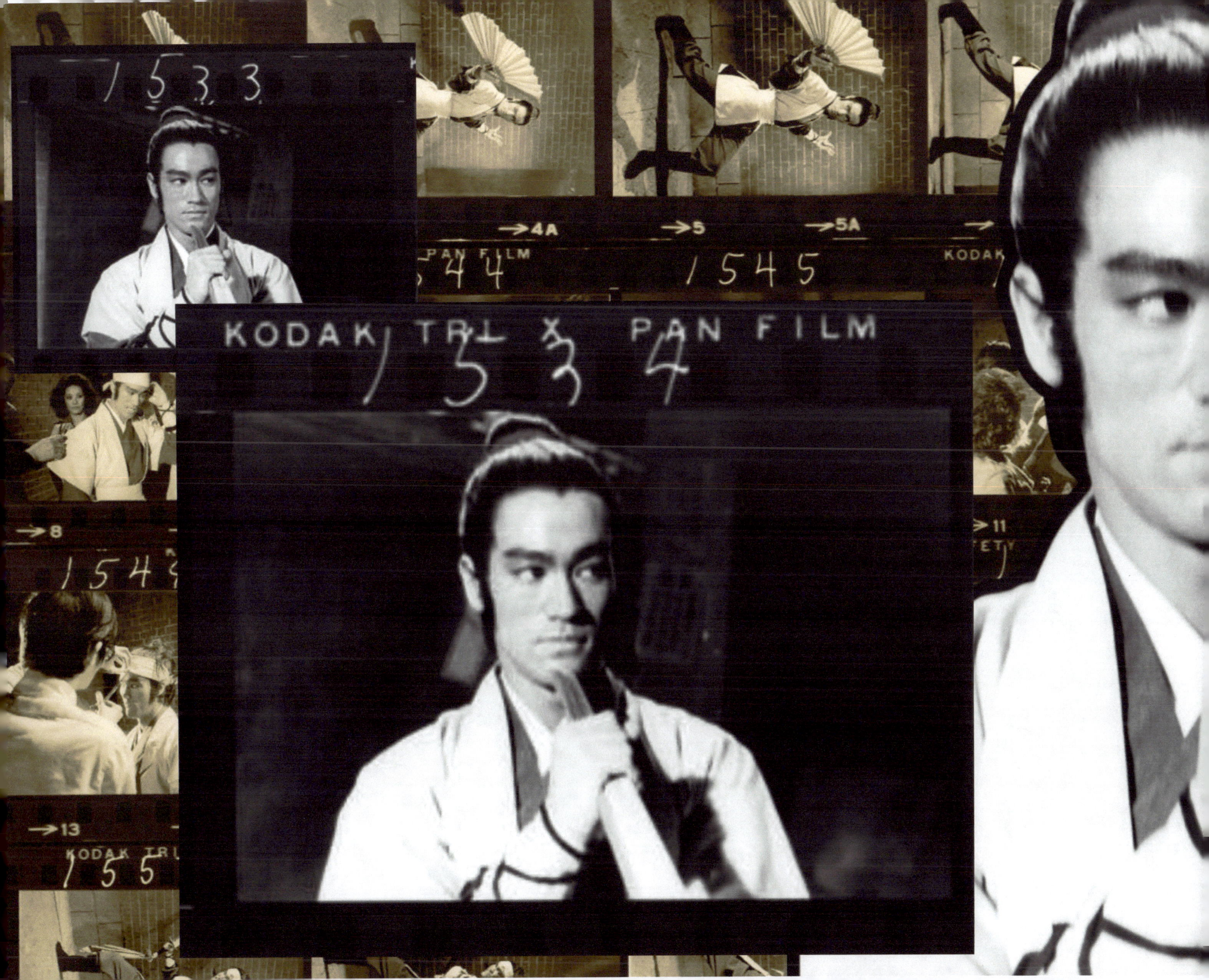

1533
1545
KODAK TRI X PAN FILM
1534
1549
1555
4A
5
5A
8
11
13
KODAK

FILM
1542
1545
KODAK SAFETY FILM
1546
5
5A
6
6A
7
7A
13
13A
KODAK TRI X PAN
1553

A YOUNG SAMMO HUNG HELPS WITH BRUCE'S WARDROBE

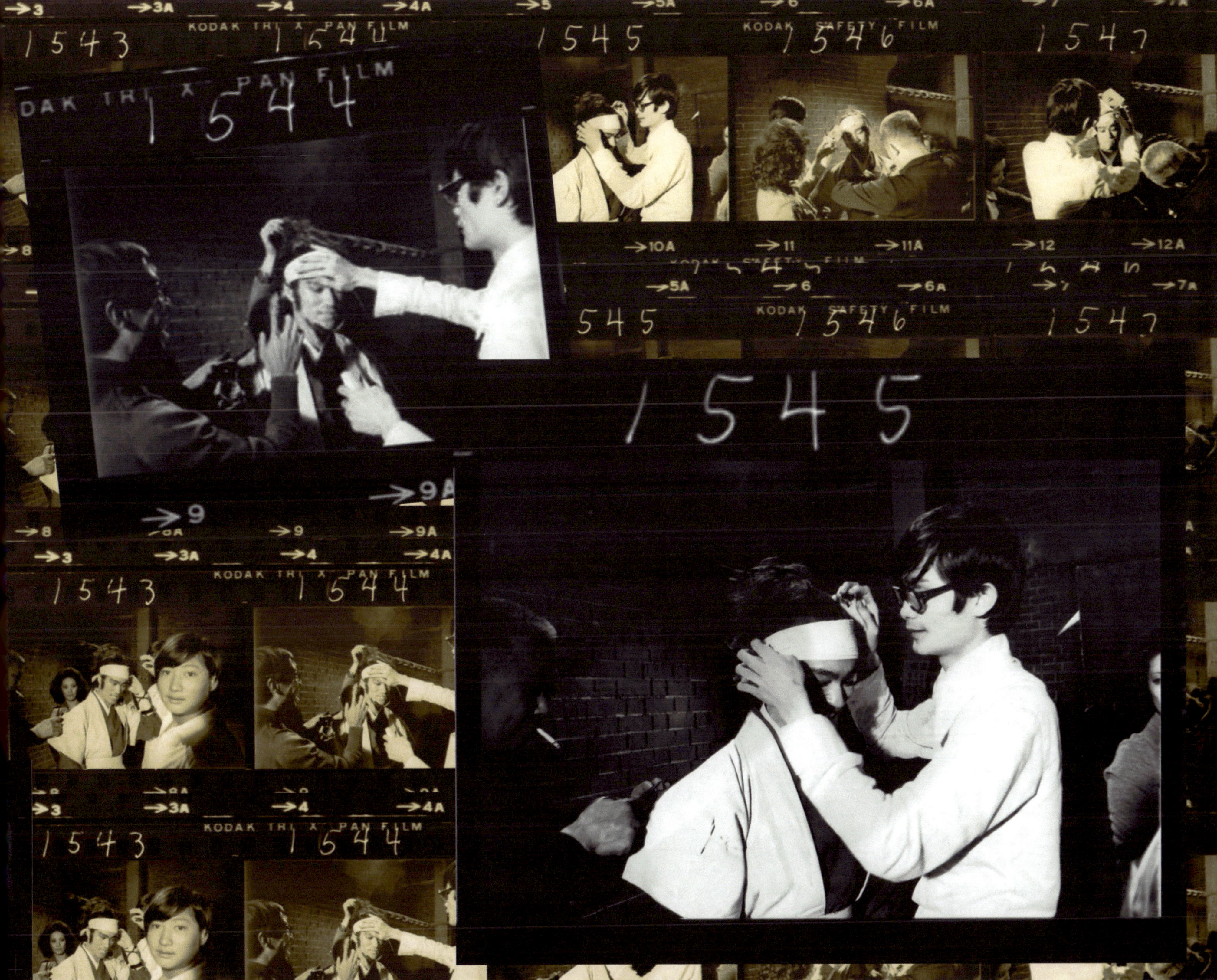

KODAK TRI X PAN FILM
1543
1544
1545
1546
1547
KODAK SAFETY FILM
1545
545
1546
1547
1545
KODAK TRI X PAN FILM
1543
1544
1543
1544

1543
1544
1545
1546
1547
KODAK TRI X PAN FILM
KODAK SAFETY FILM
SAFETY FILM
1546
KODAK SAFETY FILM
546

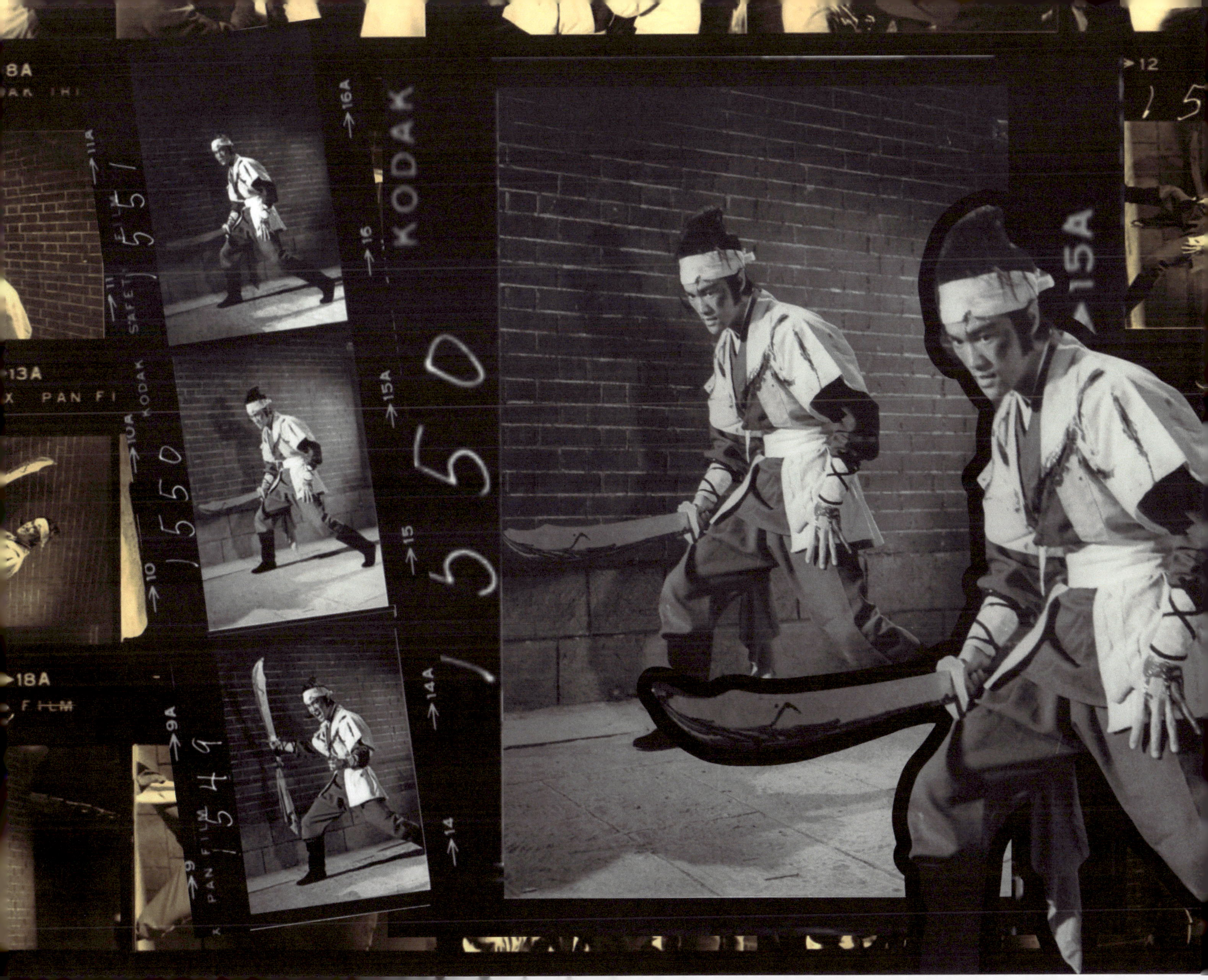

KODAK
1550
1551
1549
15A

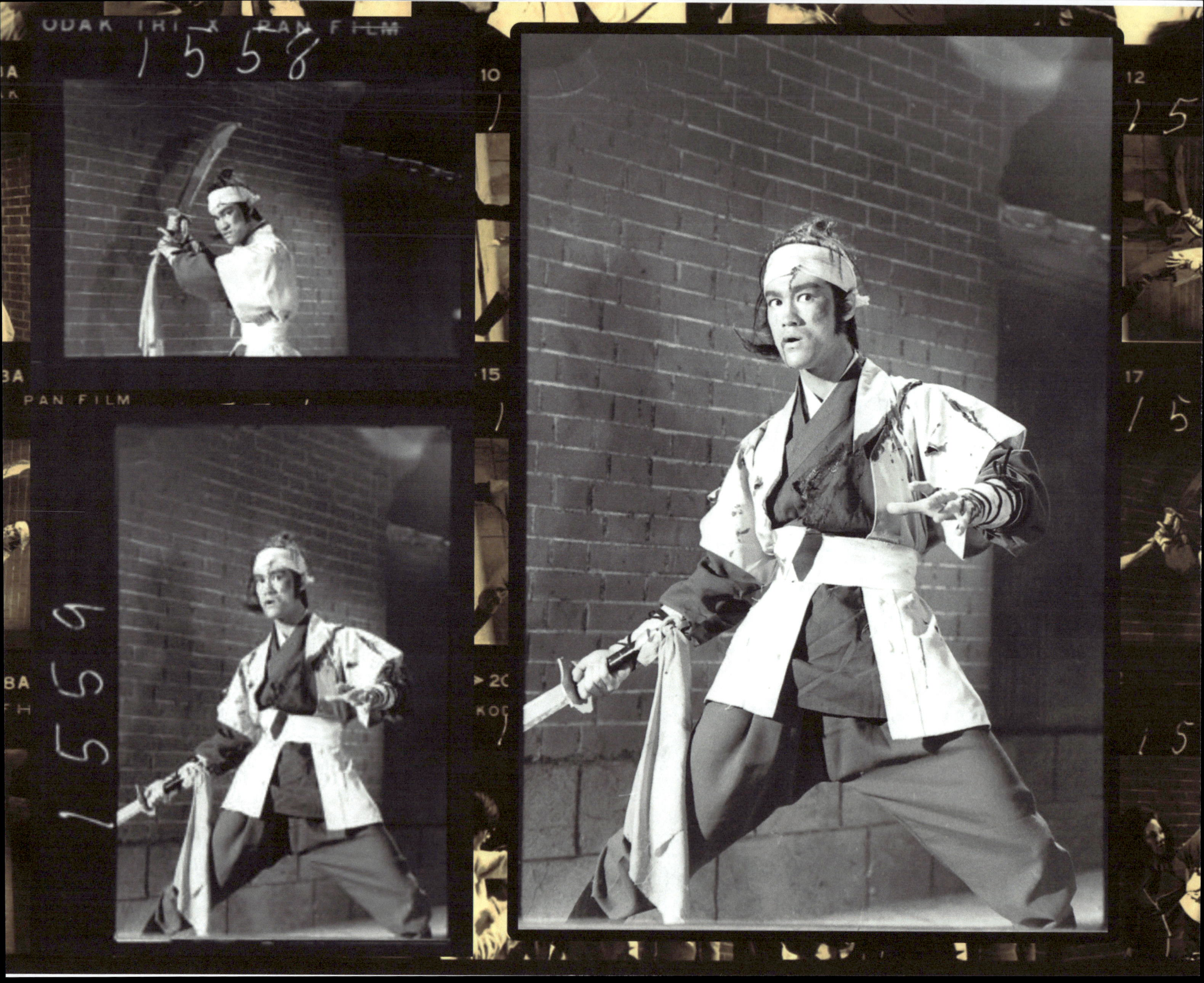
ODAK TRI-X PAN FILM
1558
PAN FILM
1559

KODAK SAFETY FILM
1560
1561
9
12
X PAN FILM
PAN FILM
14
14A
15
15A
16
16A
17
8A
19
22
FILM

WARRIOR SHOOT – COLOUR SHOTS

A SELECTION OF COLOUR PHOTOS BY CHAN YUK.
BRUCE LEE'S PHOTOGRAPHER CAPTURED TIMELESS WARRIOR SHOOT MOMENTS.
RARE BLACK AND WHITE TREASURES SIT ALONGSIDE COLOUR.
FANS TREASURE THESE IMAGES OF BRUCE'S UNIQUE OUTFITS.
FULL COLOUR REVEALS TEXTURE, TONE, AND DETAIL.
THESE SHOTS ADORNED THE COVERS OF COUNTLESS MARTIAL ARTS MAGAZINES.
POWERFUL IMAGERY SHOWS BRUCE BEYOND THE MOVIE SCREEN PERSONA.
HERE, BRUCE RADIATES STRENGTH, PRESENCE, AND CHARISMA.
MANY WISHED THIS CHARACTER HAD MADE IT TO THE BIG SCREEN.
PHOTOS PRESERVE VISIONS OF BRUCE'S ALTERNATIVE WARRIOR PATH.
CHAN YUK'S ARTISTRY GIVES BRUCE STRIKING LIVING REALISM.
THE SESSION HIGHLIGHTS DISCIPLINE, POWER, AND GRACEFUL EXPRESSION.
EVERY FRAME REFLECTS BRUCE'S ENDURING WARRIOR SPIRIT.
THIS COLLECTION REMAINS TREASURED BY FANS WORLDWIDE.
IMMORTAL IMAGES CAPTURE THE ESSENCE OF MARTIAL LEGEND.

THE WARRIOR SHOOT

THE WARRIOR SHOOT

THE WARRIOR SHOOT

THE WARRIOR SHOOT

THE WARRIOR SHOOT

THE WARRIOR SHOOT

THE WARRIOR SHOOT

THE WARRIOR SHOOT

THE WARRIOR SHOOT

Bruce Lee at Shaw Brothers, 1972 Moment

In 1972 Bruce Lee made bold moves.
At his peak, he challenged Hong Kong cinema.
He needed financing for his next big project.
Raymond Chow of Golden Harvest hesitated support.
Bruce stepped into rival Shaw Brothers studios.
There he tried costumes, performed striking screen tests.
Images soon appeared across the Hong Kong press.
Bruce in period garb, fierce and commanding presence.
The message was loud, clear, and undeniable.
Chow feared losing his greatest star to Shaw.
Golden Harvest moved quickly, financing Game of Death.
The photographs remain a fascinating cinematic "what if."
Not mere tests, but history captured in stills.
Bruce balanced between studios, shaping his legacy.
These moments echo through martial arts film history.

我一向喜歡苗可秀。

BRUCE
LEE
FOREVER
Peace. Love. Brotherhood
Bruce Lee

SPECIAL THANK YOU TO
TIM HOLLINGSWORTH
AND THE WORK HE DOES FOR
EASTERN HEROES

www.ingramcontent.com/pod-product-compliance
Lightning Source LLC
Chambersburg PA
CBHW041119010826

48981CB00034BA/450